Polly Hopper's Pouch

by Louise Bonnett-Rampersaud

illustrated by Lina Chesak-Liberace

DUTTON CHILDREN'S BOOKS · NEW YORK

Text copyright © 2001 by Louise Bonnett-Rampersaud
Illustrations copyright © 2001 by Lina Chesak
All rights reserved.

CIP Data is available.

Published in the United States 2001 by Dutton Children's Books,
a division of Penguin Putnam Books for Young Readers
345 Hudson Street, New York, New York 10014
www.penguinputnam.com
Designed by Ellen M. Lucaire
Printed in Hong Kong
First Edition
ISBN 0-525-46525-1
1 3 5 7 9 10 8 6 4 2

Polly Hopper was a curious kangaroo.

She wondered why she could jump
so much higher than anyone else.

And how far the field stretched.

She wondered how many stars twinkled at night.

And where the trains that chugged by were going.

She wondered how Topper Hopper, her charming husband,

could dance so well with his big, floppy feet.

But most of all, she wondered why
she had a shopping bag on her tummy.

None of the other creatures she knew had one.
She looked at the emus. They didn't have one.

She looked at the rabbits. They didn't have one.

She looked at the dingoes. They didn't have one, either.

The other ladies she saw all carried handbags,
which weren't like her shopping bag at all.

What good is it?
Polly wondered as she stared at her tummy.

"Stop wondering," said an elderly kangaroo.
"One day you'll know why you have that lovely pouch."

Pouch? thought Polly.
She didn't think it was lovely.

Her books from the library were too heavy to go in it.

Her loaves of bread were too wide to fit in it.

Her peaches got lost in the bottom.

And even the flowers from her garden didn't fit right.
They just flopped over the top.

But the elderly kangaroo had told her that
one day she would know. So she waited.

And waited.

And finally that day came.
Polly and Topper Hopper had a little baby of their own.
They named their soft, sweet baby kangaroo Minny Hopper.

Polly Hopper's pouch was the best
possible place for Minny. She fit perfectly.

Her head rested gently there.
She stayed nice and warm inside it.

And as she grew, her face peeked out
just enough for her to see her new world.

"This isn't a shopping bag after all,"
exclaimed Polly Hopper.

"It's a wonderful place to
keep my baby safe and warm."

And every night, as Minny Hopper closed her eyes
and fell asleep, Polly reached down, gave her a kiss, and
declared that it *was* a lovely pouch after all.